Rub a Dub Dub

Rub a Dub Dub

As told by **Kin Eagle**

Illustrated by **Rob Gilbert**

WHISPERING COYOTE PRESS
Dallas

A *Kids at Our House* Book

Published by Whispering Coyote Press
300 Crescent Court, Suite 860, Dallas, TX 75201

Text copyright © 1999 by Kin Eagle
Illustrations copyright © 1999 by Rob Gilbert

Text was set in 16-point Tiffany Medium.
Book production and design by *The Kids at Our House*
10 9 8 7 6 5 4 3 2 1
Printed in Hong Kong

Library of Congress Cataloging–in–Publication Data

Eagle, Kin.
Rub a dub dub / retold by Kin Eagle ; illustrated by Rob Gilbert.
p.   cm.
Summary: This expanded version of the traditional rhyme shows
what happens to the butcher, the baker, and the candlestick maker
when they go fishing in their tub.
ISBN 1-58089-008-3(hc)
[1. Fishing—Fiction. 2. Characters in literature—Fiction. 3. Stories in rhyme.] I. Gilbert,
Roby, 1966- ill. II. Title.
PZ8.3.E112515Ru 1998
[E]—dc21   98-14729
                                                          CIP
                                                           AC

For my Dad,
the greatest man I've ever known
—K.E.

To Danny and Kim, with love
—R.G.

Rub a dub dub
Three men in a tub
and who do you think they be?
The butcher, the baker,
the candlestick maker,
Turn 'em out, fishermen three.

Their wives sent them out,
for some salmon or trout,
for dinner on Saturday night.
But while in their tub
as they fished for some grub,
they suffered a terrible fright!

They snagged one so large
it was rocking their barge
as they all but fell out, being tossed.

First he dragged them around,
far away from the ground,
then he left them just floating there, lost.

As they were afloat
in their small wooden boat
and wondering how to get home,
they were tossed by the waves
trying hard to be brave
on currents all blue green with foam.

But suddenly, trouble—
"Look men, on the double!"
the butcher screamed, though he was meek.
"Cup your hands without fail,
and use them to bail!
Help! Our tub has just sprung a big leak!"

The baker cried, "Wait!
I've an idea that's great!"
As he laughed with his hand on his head.

"With my tools and my oven,
and US as the stuffin',
we'll float home in hollowed out bread!"

The candlestick man
cried, "That's a *bad* plan!
We don't have the things you require!
But if we act quick
with my big candlestick,
I can build us a signalling fire!"

The butcher screamed, "No!
We'll burn, don't you know!
Besides, you've forgotten the catch:
You might know how to handle
a fire and candle,
but the baker just dropped the last match!"

Then the butcher and baker
and candlestick maker
saw water was filling their tub,
"Hurry up! Start to think,
Or we surely will sink!
And ride a convertible sub!"

Fiddle-dee-dee
First one, then all three,
were laughing as hard as you please.
In all of their bother
They forgot that the water
was only as high as their knees!

And so they *walked* home
through bluish green foam,
but they did not shout, scream or yell.
They were feeling so silly,
acting all willy-nilly,
and decided it best not to tell.

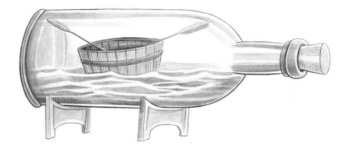

Rub a Dub Dub

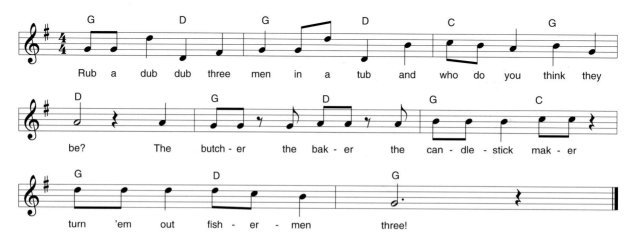

Rub a dub dub three men in a tub and who do you think they be? The butch-er the bak-er the can-dle-stick mak-er turn 'em out fish-er-men three!

2. Their wives sent them out,
   for some salmon or trout,
   for dinner on Saturday night.
   But while in their tub
   as they fished for some grub,
   they suffered a terrible fright!

3. They snagged one so large
   it was rocking their barge
   as they all but fell out, being tossed.
   First he dragged them around,
   far away from the ground,
   then he left them just floating there, lost.

4. As they were afloat
   in their small wooden boat
   and wondering how to get home,
   they were tossed by the waves
   trying hard to be brave
   on currents all blue green with foam.

5. But suddenly, trouble—
   "Look men, on the double!"
   the butcher screamed, though he was meek.
   "Cup your hands without fail,
   and use them to bail!
   Help! Our tub has just sprung a big leak!"

6. The baker cried, "Wait!
   I've an idea that's great!"
   As he laughed with his hand on his head.
   "With my tools and my oven,
   and US as the stuffin',
   we'll float home in hollowed out bread!"

7. The candlestick man
   cried, "That's a BAD plan!
   We don't have the things you require!
   But if we act quick
   with my big candlestick,
   I can build us a signalling fire!"

8. The butcher screamed, "No!
   We'll burn, don't you know!
   Besides, you've forgotten the catch:
   You might know how to handle
   a fire and candle,
   but the baker just dropped the last match!"

9. Then the butcher and baker
   and candlestick maker
   saw water was filling their tub.
   "Hurry up! Start to think,
   Or we surely will sink!
   And ride a convertible sub!"

10. Fiddle-dee-dee
    First one, then all three,
    were laughing as hard as you please.
    In all of their bother
    They forgot that the water
    was only as high as their knees!

11. And so they *walked* home
    through bluish green foam,
    but they did not shout, scream or yell.
    They were feeling so silly,
    acting all willy-nilly,
    and decided it best not to tell.